Move Over, ROVER!

Move Over, ROVER!

Karen Beaumont

Illustrated by
Jane Dyer

SCHOLASTIC INC.
New York Toronto London Auckland Sydney
Mexico City New Delhi Hong Kong Buenos Aires

Rover's in the doghouse,
chewing on a bone.
What a day to romp and play!
Too bad he's all alone.

Oh, my, look at the sky!
Thunder! Lightning!
Mighty frightening!

Rain is pouring....
Oh, how boring.

Rover's in the doghouse,
sleeping through the storm....
Cat is looking all around
to find a place that's warm.

Move over, Rover!

Cat's in the doghouse,
sleeping through the storm. . . .
Raccoon is looking all around
to find a place that's warm.

Skit-scat, Cat!
Move over, Rover!

Raccoon's in the doghouse,
sleeping through the storm....
Squirrel is looking all around
to find a place that's warm.

Make room, Raccoon!
Skit-scat, Cat!
Move over, Rover!

Squirrel's in the doghouse,
sleeping through the storm. . . .
Blue Jay's looking all around
to find a place that's warm.

Squeeze in, Squirrel!
Make room, Raccoon!
Skit-scat, Cat!
Move over, Rover!

Blue Jay's in the doghouse,
sleeping through the storm....
Snake is looking all around
to find a place that's warm.

Out of the way, Blue Jay!
Squeeze in, Squirrel!
Make room, Raccoon!
Skit-scat, Cat!
Move over, Rover!

Snake's in the doghouse,
sleeping through the storm....
Mouse is looking all around
to find a place that's warm.

Slide aside, Snake!
Out of the way, Blue Jay!
Squeeze in, Squirrel!
Make room, Raccoon!
Skit-scat, Cat!
Move over, Rover!

Tight fit. Might split.
Sorry, Mouse. Full house!

Crowded in the doghouse,
all are sleeping well.
But then…sniff, sniff!
They catch a whiff!
What's that awful smell?

Skitter, scatter!
What's the matter?
Scamper, scurry!
What's the hurry?

Skunk's in the doghouse,
sleeping through the storm....
The rest are racing round to find
another place that's warm.

Oh, my, look at the sky!
Storm's over.
Where's Rover?

Romping? Racing?

Jumping?

No!

Chasing?

Rover's in the doghouse,
chewing on a bone.
Soaked and sopping,
tail flip-flopping,
happy he's alone!

For my Uncle Bill,
with love and gratitude
—K. B.

For Woolly
—J. D.

ISBN-13: 978-0-545-15506-9
ISBN-10: 0-545-15506-1

Text copyright © 2006 by Karen Beaumont.
Illustrations copyright © 2006 by Jane Dyer.
All rights reserved. Published by Scholastic Inc.,
557 Broadway, New York, NY 10012, by arrangement with
Houghton Mifflin Harcourt Publishing Company.
SCHOLASTIC and associated logos are trademarks
and/or registered trademarks of Scholastic Inc.

12 11 10 9 8 7 6 5 4   9 10 11 12 13 14/0

Printed in the U.S.A.   40

First Scholastic printing, January 2009

The illustrations in this book were done in watercolor and
liquid acrylic on Arches 140 lb. hot press watercolor paper.
The display type was hand lettered by Judythe Sieck.
The text type was set in Memphis.
Designed by Lauren Rille